WHOLE WIDE WORLD

PETRA

by Kristine Spanier, MLIS

pogo

Ideas for Parents and Teachers

Pogo Books let children practice reading informational text while introducing them to nonfiction features such as headings, labels, sidebars, maps, and diagrams, as well as a table of contents, glossary, and index.

Carefully leveled text with a strong photo match offers early fluent readers the support they need to succeed.

Before Reading

- "Walk" through the book and point out the various nonfiction features. Ask the student what purpose each feature serves.
- Look at the glossary together. Read and discuss the words.

Read the Book

- Have the child read the book independently.
- Invite him or her to list questions that arise from reading.

After Reading

- Discuss the child's questions. Talk about how he or she might find answers to those questions.
- Prompt the child to think more. Ask: Did you know about Petra before you read this book? What more would you like to learn?

Pogo Books are published by Jump!
5357 Penn Avenue South
Minneapolis, MN 55419
www.jumplibrary.com

Library of Congress Cataloging-in-Publication Data

Names: Spanier, Kristine, author.
Title: Petra / by Kristine Spanier.
Description: Minneapolis, MN: Jump!, Inc., [2021]
Series: Whole wide world | Includes index.
Audience: Ages 7-10 | Audience: Grades 2-3
Identifiers: LCCN 2020030696 (print)
LCCN 2020030697 (ebook)
ISBN 9781645277477 (hardcover)
ISBN 9781645277484 (paperback)
ISBN 9781645277491 (ebook)
Subjects: LCSH: Petra (Extinct city)–Juvenile literature.
Jordan–Antiquities–Juvenile literature.
Classification: LCC DS154.9.P48 S63 2021 (print)
LCC DS154.9.P48 (ebook) | DDC 939.4/8–dc23
LC record available at https://lccn.loc.gov/2020030696
LC ebook record available at https://lccn.loc.gov/2020030697

Editor: Jenna Gleisner
Designer: Molly Ballanger

Photo Credits: evenfh/Shutterstock, cover; Andreas Wolochow/Shutterstock, 1; Rawpixel.com/Shutterstock, 3; volkova natalia/Shutterstock, 4; Dr_Flash/Shutterstock, 5; Ralf Siemieniec/Shutterstock, 6-7; Anton_Ivanov/Shutterstock, 8; Matyas Rehak/Shutterstock, 9; vvoe/Shutterstock, 10-11; Yongyut Kumsri/Shutterstock, 12-13; Juergen Ritterbach/Alamy, 14-15; Cezary Wojtkowski/Shutterstock, 16-17; Natiur/Dreamstime, 18; Petr Honeger/EyeEm/Getty, 19; ClickAlps/Mauritius/SuperStock, 20-21; travelwild/Shutterstock, 23.

Printed in the United States of America at Corporate Graphics in North Mankato, Minnesota.

TABLE OF CONTENTS

CHAPTER 1
Rose-Red City....................4

CHAPTER 2
Rock Structures....................8

CHAPTER 3
Petra Today....................18

QUICK FACTS & TOOLS
At a Glance....................22
Glossary....................23
Index....................24
To Learn More....................24

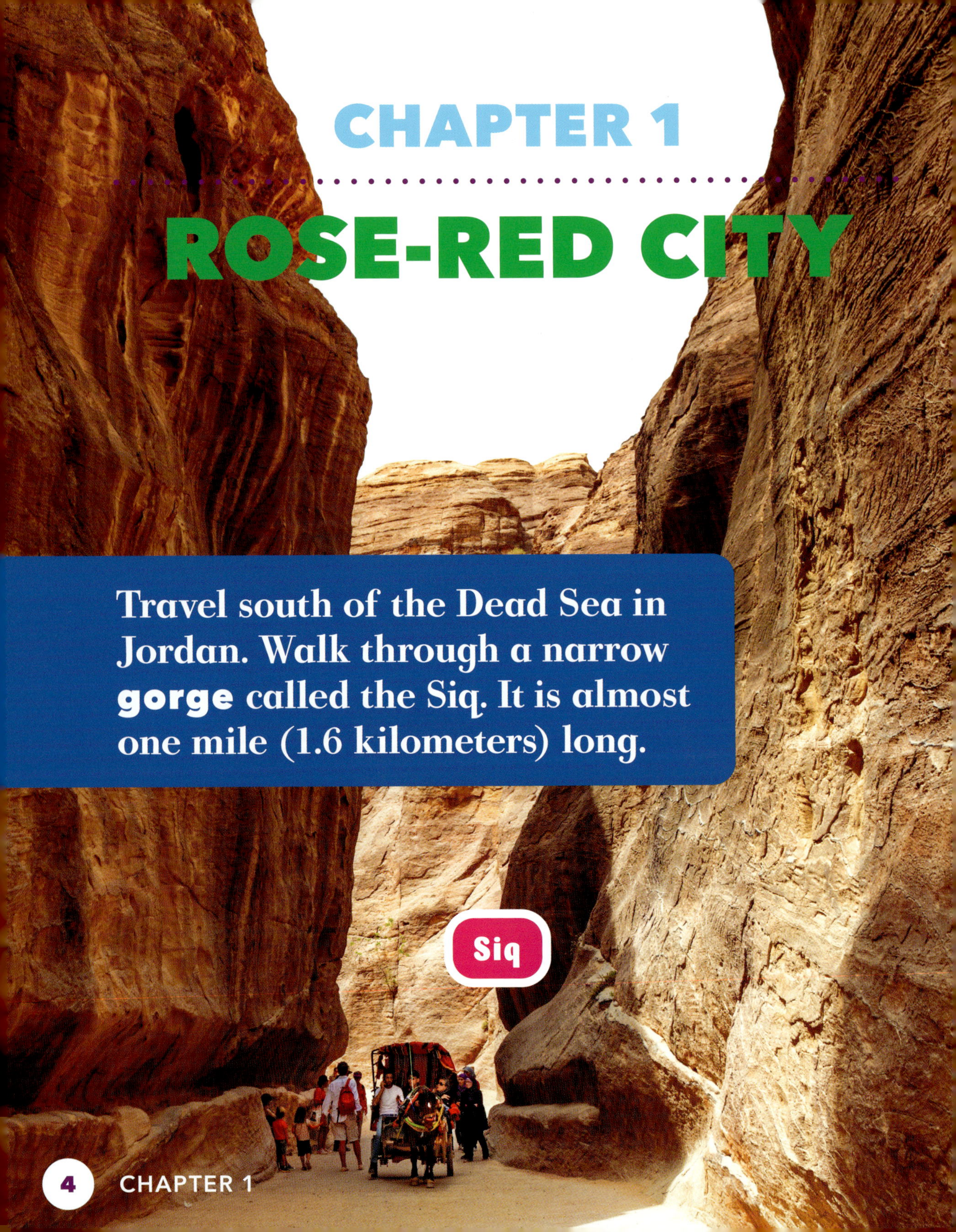

CHAPTER 1

ROSE-RED CITY

Travel south of the Dead Sea in Jordan. Walk through a narrow **gorge** called the Siq. It is almost one mile (1.6 kilometers) long.

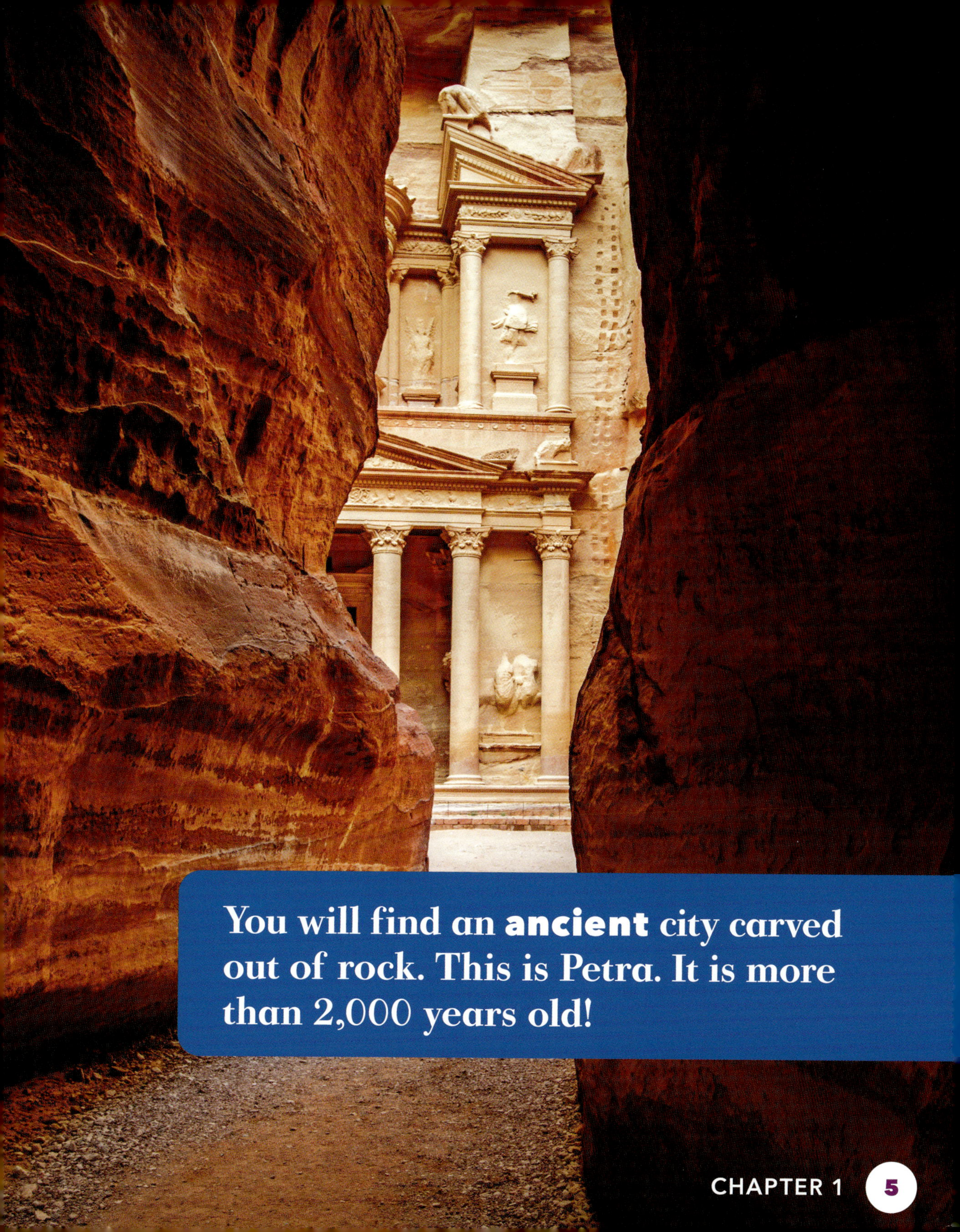

You will find an **ancient** city carved out of rock. This is Petra. It is more than 2,000 years old!

Petra means "rock" in Greek. People call it the rose-red city. Why? The **structures** are carved out of red sandstone.

Petra was a **capital** in the 400s BCE. The Nabataean **Kingdom** ruled. This was an Arab **tribe**. More than 30,000 people lived in this desert area.

WHAT DO YOU THINK?

People here collected rainwater. It moved through channels and pipes. It was used for farming. What else do you think they used it for?

CHAPTER 2

ROCK STRUCTURES

More than 800 structures have been found here. Large groups of people met at the Ad Deir. This was a place of **worship**. The doorway is 26 feet (7.9 meters) tall!

Ad Deir

The **Tomb** of the Roman Soldier was next to a ballroom. People had feasts in the ballroom. They **honored** the dead.

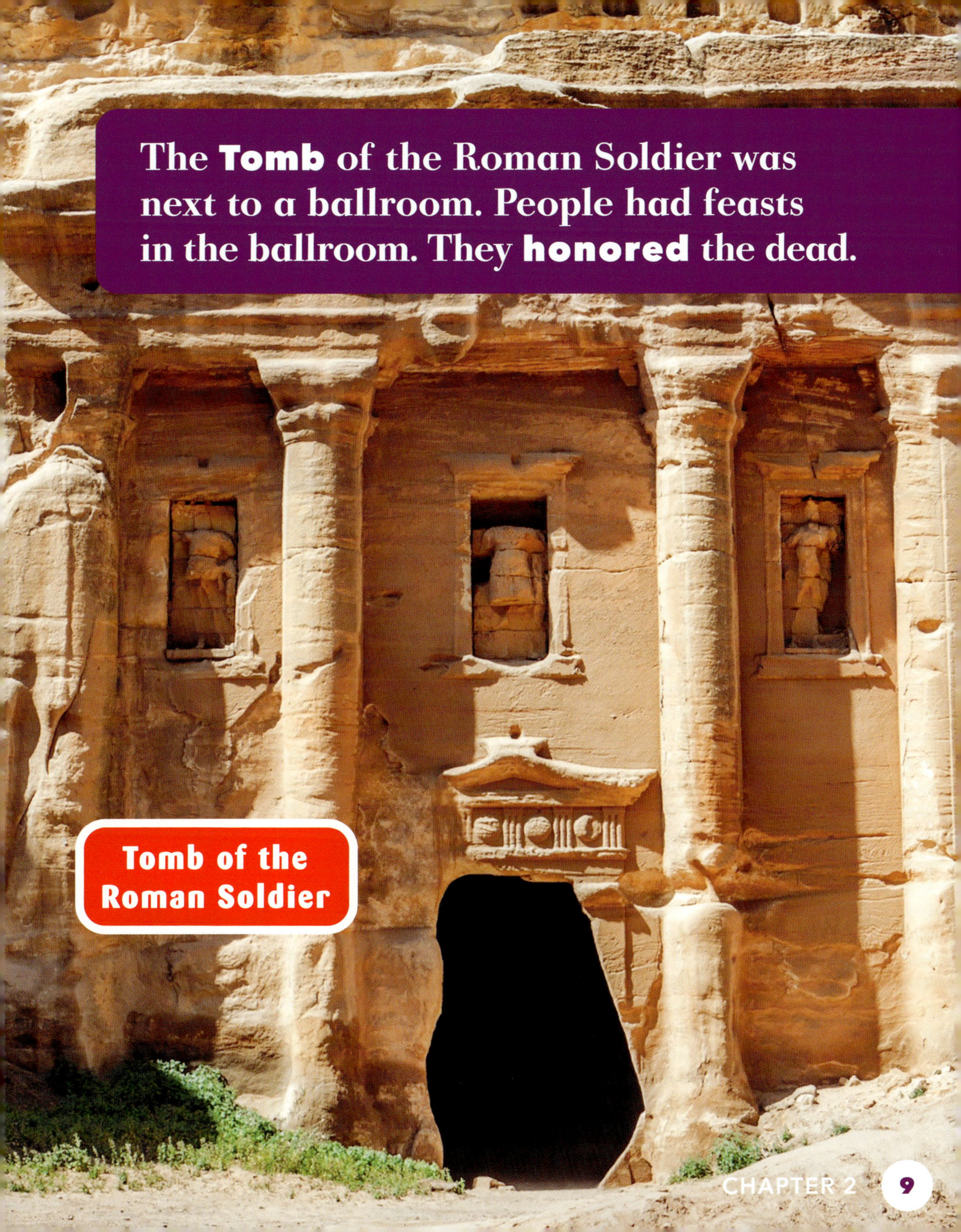

Tomb of the Roman Soldier

An **urn** carving sits at the top of the Urn Tomb. A king may have been buried here. Later, it was used as a church. Some think it may have also been used as a courthouse.

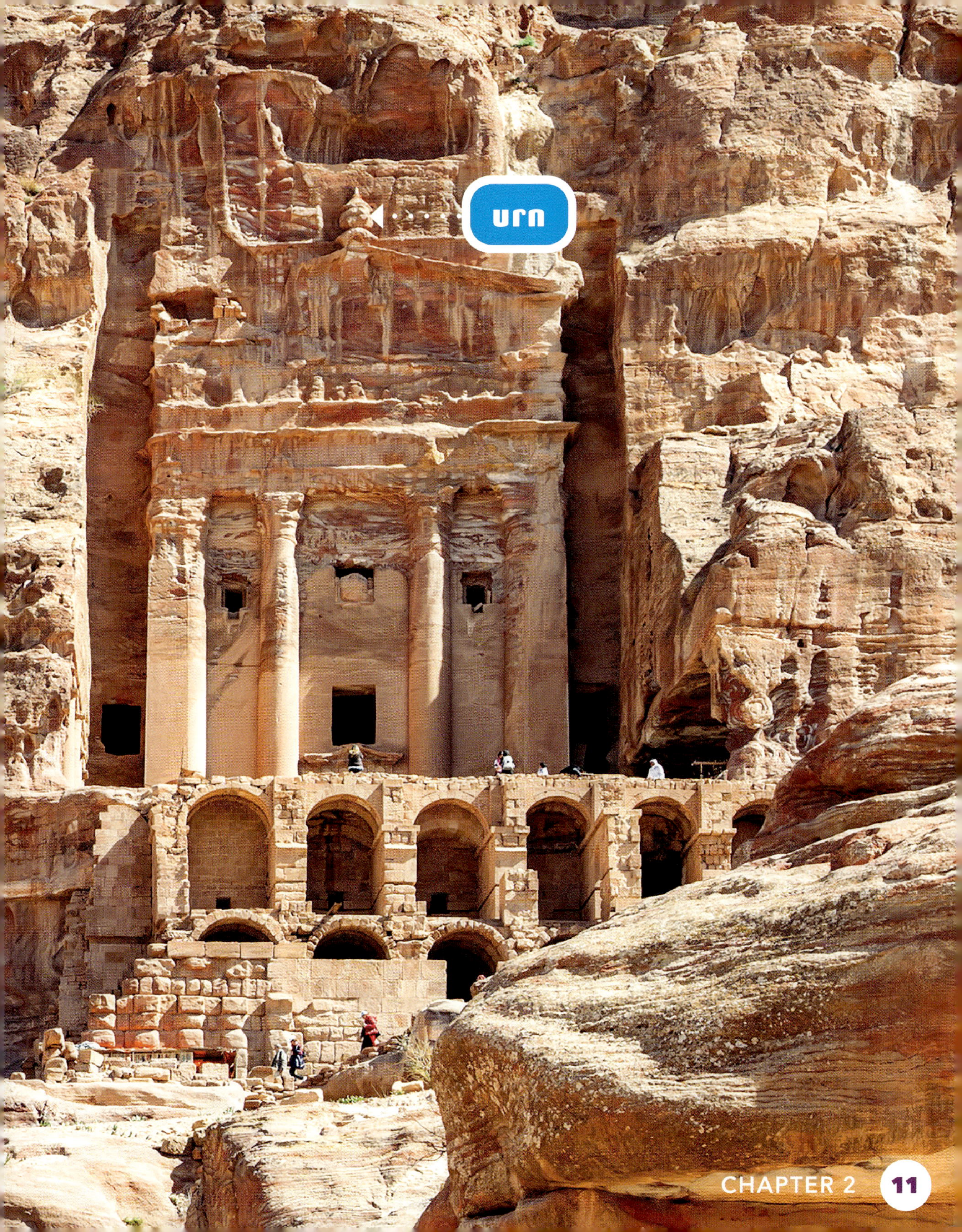
urn

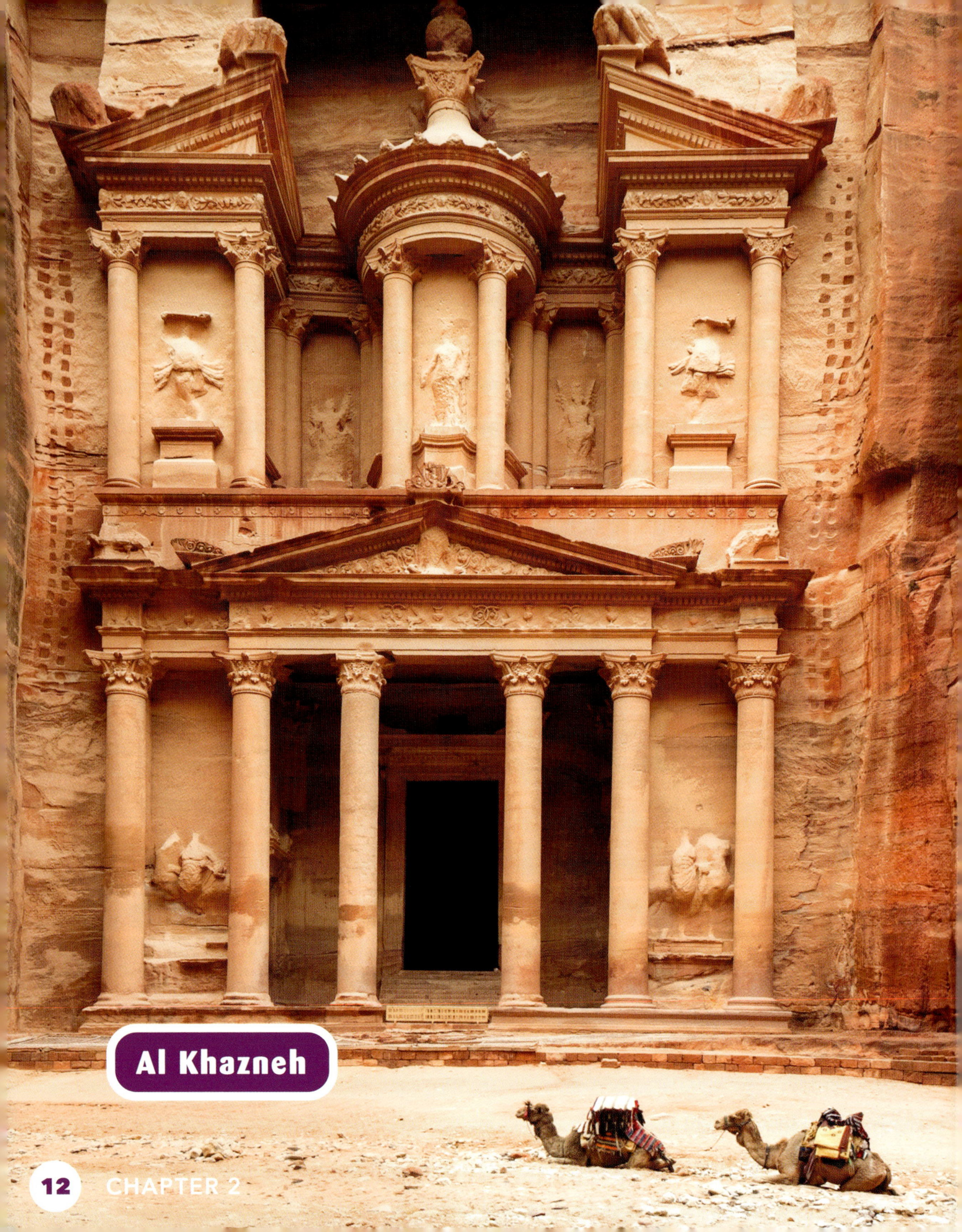

Al Khazneh

The Al Khazneh is 141 feet (43 m) high. It has three stone rooms. Some say it was a library. Others say it was a tomb for a king. Some think treasure was kept inside. It is still a mystery.

WHAT DO YOU THINK?

It is hard to know for sure what each building was used for. **Archaeologists** work here. They continue to uncover ancient buildings. They find clues. Would you like this job? Why or why not?

The Palace Tomb is 151 feet (46 m) tall. It is 161 feet (49 m) wide. This makes it one of the largest structures in Petra. Twelve large columns line the bottom. There are 18 more on top. Inside are four burial chambers. No one knows who was buried in them.

column
Palace Tomb

theater

The city even had a theater. It could fit 8,000 people. The rows face north and east. Why? This was so the sun would not shine in the audience's eyes!

DID YOU KNOW?

Johann Ludwig Burckhardt was a Swiss explorer. People living near Petra showed him the city in 1812. He introduced it to the rest of the world.

CHAPTER 3

PETRA TODAY

People can visit Petra. But they must be careful. Why? Sandstone is fragile. Even wind and water can damage it.

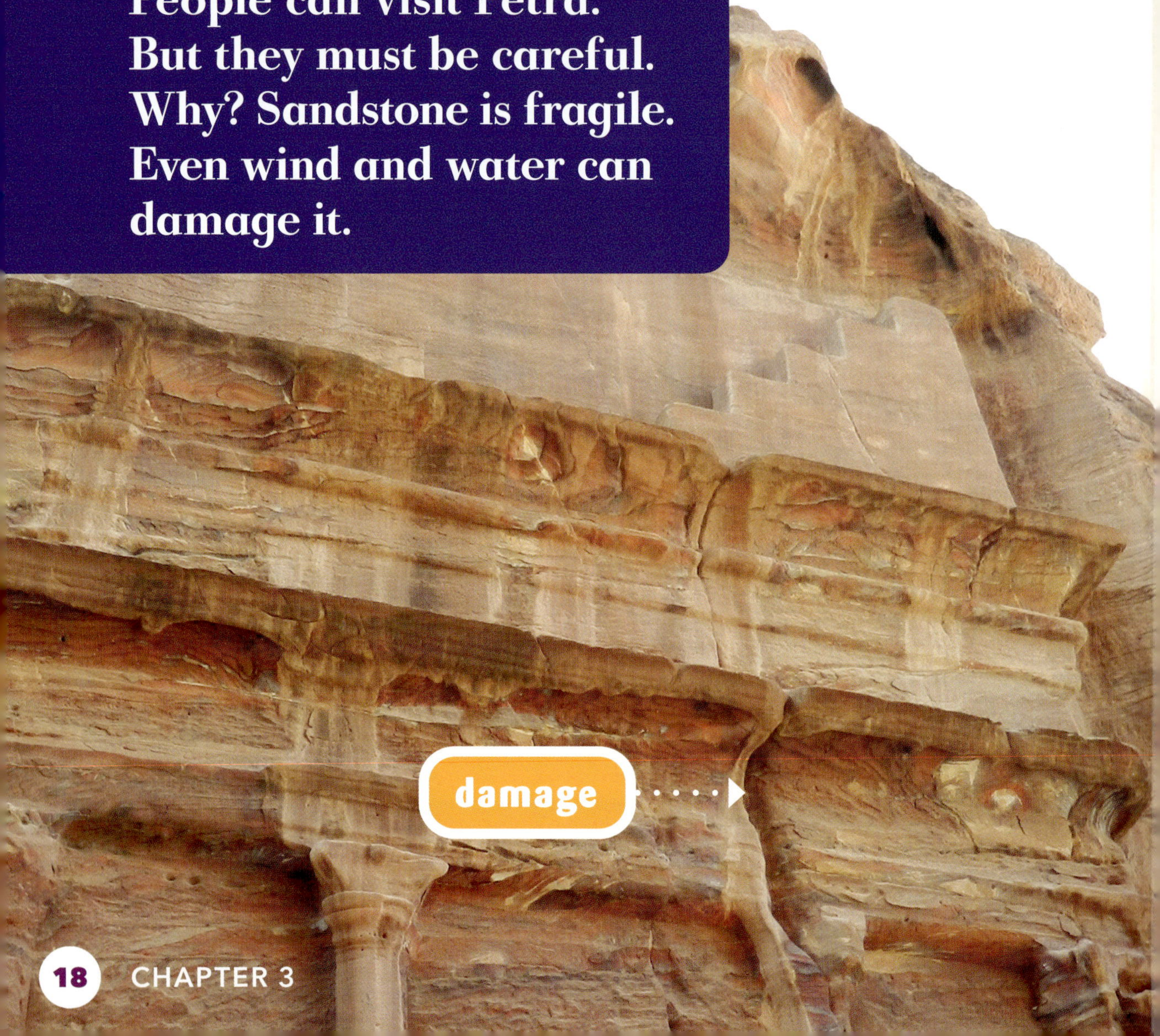

Visitors should not litter or leave graffiti. They also should not lean on the walls.

TAKE A LOOK!

Many groups of people have lived in Petra. Who were they?

400s BCE
Petra is the Nabataean capital.

106 CE
Romans take control of Petra.

300s CE
Petra becomes a Christian city.

600s CE
Petra becomes a Muslim city.

1100s
Crusaders take over Petra.

1200s to PRESENT
Arab tribes live in and around Petra.

Petra will continue to be a place of wonder if we care for it today. Would you like to explore Petra?

QUICK FACTS & TOOLS

AT A GLANCE

PETRA

Location: Jordan

Size: 102 square miles (264 square km)

Years Built: around 100 BCE to 100 CE

Primary Architects: Nabataean people

Past Use: Nabataean capital

Current Use: cultural site and visitor attraction

Number of Visitors Each Year: around 1.1 million

GLOSSARY

ancient: Belonging to a period long ago.

archaeologists: People who study the distant past, which often involves digging up old buildings, objects, and bones and examining them carefully.

capital: The city in a country or state where the government is based.

Crusaders: Soldiers who took part in Christian military expeditions.

gorge: A deep valley.

honored: Showed respect.

kingdom: An area that is associated with or under the control of a person or king.

structures: Things that have been built.

tomb: A grave, room, or building that holds a dead body.

tribe: A large group of related people that shares the same language, customs, and laws, and usually lives in the same area.

urn: A vase with a base or pedestal that is used as an ornament or container.

worship: The act of showing love and devotion to a god or gods, especially by praying or singing in a religious building with others.

INDEX

Ad Deir 8
Al Khazneh 13
Arab tribe 6, 20
archaeologists 13
ballroom 9
Burckhardt, Johann Ludwig 17
church 10
courthouse 10
Crusaders 20
Dead Sea 4
desert 6
farming 6
Jordan 4
library 13
Nabataean Kingdom 6, 20
Palace Tomb 14
Romans 20
sandstone 6, 18
Siq 4
structures 6, 8, 14
theater 17
Tomb of the Roman Soldier 9
Urn Tomb 10
visitors 19

TO LEARN MORE

Finding more information is as easy as 1, 2, 3.

1. Go to www.factsurfer.com
2. Enter "Petra" into the search box.
3. Choose your book to see a list of websites.

FACT SURFER